The ArtScroll Children's Holiday Series

Yaffa Ganz

YOM KIPPUR

WITH BINA, BENNY AND CHAGGAI HAYONAH

Illustrated by Liat Benyaminy Ariel

© *Copyright 1991, by* MESORAH PUBLICATIONS, Ltd. *and* YAFFA GANZ
4401 Second Avenue / Brooklyn, N.Y. 11232 / (718) 921-9000
Produced by SEFERCRAFT, INC. */ Brooklyn, N.Y.*

halom! I'm Chaggai Hayonah — Chaggai the Holiday Dove. It's that special time of the year again, *bein keseh l'asor* — between Rosh Hashanah and Yom Kippur. My friends Bina and Benny are very busy trying to be better than they were last year. In fact, they're trying to be the very best they possibly can, because these are the *Aseres Yemei Teshuvah* — the Ten Days of Repentance.

"It's our last chance before Yom Kippur to show G-d we're really sorry for all the things we did wrong last year!" said Benny. "I've been doing as many *mitzvos* as I can think of. I wonder if I forgot anything?"

Bina laughed. "You're so busy being sorry that you forgot to apologize for taking my pen without p rmission and then losing it!"

Benny smiled. "Wow! How could I forget that! I really am sorry, Bina. I know you liked that pen and I shouldn't have taken it without asking you, but you weren't here and I couldn't find my own pen and I just had to do my homework. I'm sorry."

"Never mind," said Bina. "Imma said she'd buy me another one."

"It's a good thing you reminded me to apologize and ask for *mechilah*," said Benny. "*Hashem* doesn't forgive us for bad things we did to other people unless the people forgive us first!"

Wouldn't it be nice, Benny, if we could remember to do everything right all the time? Then maybe we wouldn't need Yom Kippur."

"Maybe, but it's awfully hard to be perfect all the time. There are so many *mitzvos* to do, and so many things we shouldn't do."

"It's a good thing we can always do *teshuvah*," said Bina. "*Teshuvah* means that even if you do something wrong, you can change it. If you're really sorry for having done an *aveirah*, you must say with your full heart what you have done, that you are sorry for doing it, and that you will never do it any more. Then, if you try real hard not to do it again, it's as if you never did it in the first place. Anyone can do *teshuvah*, and everyone must do *teshuvah*, even boys or girls who aren't bar- or bas-mitzvah yet."

"I like the idea of choosing one new *mitzvah* to work on each year," said Benny. "After a few years, I'm going to have a whole collection of *mitzvos* I do just right!"

"Which *mitzvah* did you pick this year, Benny?"

"I'm going to learn part of the weekly *parashah* every day after school all by myself. What about you?"

"I'm going to try and say the *berachos* slowly so I pronounce each word."

"And I'll take the garbage out for Imma every morning without waiting until she asks me."

"And I'll be more active with *bikkur cholim* — that's the *mitzvah* of visiting and helping people who are sick. Mrs. Michaelson has very weak eyes. She just loves when youngsters come to read books for her."

Hmm . . . and I think I'll stop littering Bina and Benny's room with birdseed. I know they don't like to sweep up after I eat. And I could coo more softly in the morning so I don't wake them up . . .

on't forget there's a fast day even before Yom Kippur," said Benny. "Tzom Gedalyah is the day after Rosh Hashanah. But I never remember who Gedalyah was!"

"Neither do I," said Bina.

"Maybe Chaggai knows."

"Indeed I do!" said the dove.

Gedalyah was a very important man! When the Babylonians destroyed the First *Beis Hamikdash,* the Jews were allowed to remain in the Land of Israel. The Babylonians appointed a Jewish governor — Gedalyah ben Achikam — to rule the country. Gedalyah was a righteous and holy man, and as long as he was alive, the people lived peacefully and happily in *Eretz Yisrael.*

But then Gedalyah was murdered and the fighting began. Many Jews were killed; others ran away. The rest were taken prisoner and sent to Babylonia. *Eretz Yisrael* was in ruins. Gedalyah's death was such a great calamity that our Sages turned the day into a time of fasting and doing *teshuvah.*

 hat's so special about the tenth of Tishrei? Yom Kippur could have been any day," said Bina.

The tenth of Tishrei is a special day of forgiveness. When Moshe *Rabbeinu* came down from *Har Sinai,* he found the Jewish people worshiping a golden calf. He was so angry that he broke the *luchos,* the stone tablets with the Ten Commandments.

But G-d sent Moshe back up to the mountaintop. For two periods of forty days each, Moshe stayed there and prayed for the people. On the tenth of Tishrei he came down carrying a new set of *luchos. Hashem* had forgiven the Jews.

"Does that mean Yom Kippur is a sad day?" asked Bina.

Not at all. It's a joyous day, but a serious one. And if we're serious about doing *teshuvah* and keeping the Torah and its *mitzvos*, we can be sure that *Hashem* will forgive us, just as He forgave the Jews for the terrible sin of the Golden Calf. Knowing that makes us happy.

I know of another good day for doing *teshuvah* — on *Shabbos Shuvah* — the Shabbos between Rosh Hashanah and Yom Kippur!

hat do we do on Yom Kippur besides go to *shul*?" asked Benny.

"Let me tell you about the things we do NOT do," answered the dove.

We do not eat.

We do not drink.

We do not wash ourselves,
or use oils or creams or perfume.

We do not wear shoes made of leather.

"Once a year, on Yom Kippur, we are just like angels who don't have to worry about eating or taking care of a body! On Yom Kippur, we are busy thinking about our *neshamah*, our soul.

"I'm not sure I can manage without eating," said Benny with a worried look on his face.

"You don't have to fast the entire day," said Bina. "You aren't bar mitzvah yet."

"I know, but I'm not even sure I can fast half a day. I get hungry awfully fast!"

"Oh, Benny," cried Bina, "I know what you can do! It's a *mitzvah* to fast on Yom Kippur, but it's also a *mitzvah* to eat on Erev Yom Kippur, in order to prepare for the fast! That's one *mitzvah* you'll do very well!"

Benny's face brightened up.

"And besides eating," continued Bina, "on Erev Yom Kippur we can give *tzedakah* and ask our friends for *mechilah*. And on Yom Kippur itself, we'll fast as long as we can, and we'll *daven* carefully, and I'm sure *Hashem* will hear our prayers and seal our names in His Book of Life for a good year!"

Benny thinks he gets hungry fast. He doesn't know how quickly birds get hungry. Birds eat all day long — even doves! It's a good thing Yom Kippur is only for people!

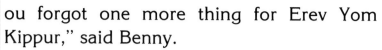ou forgot one more thing for Erev Yom Kippur," said Benny.

"I did? Let me think . . ." Bina wrinkled her nose, the way she always did when she was thinking hard. "I don't remember anything else. What did I forget?"

"*Kapparos!*" said Benny triumphantly. "Abba will bring a white rooster for himself and for me, and a white hen for Imma and you, and we'll wave the birds slowly around three times and say the prayer for *kapparos. Kapparos* means forgiveness, just like the word *Kippur*. It reminds us of the offerings the Jews used to bring in the *Beis Hamikdash* when they did something wrong."

"Just remember to hold your rooster gently! I'm always afraid someone will hurt the bird by mistake. Uncle Meyer doesn't use a live bird. He wraps money in a handkerchief and waves that instead. Then he gives the money to *tzedakah.*"

"Don't worry. I'll be careful. Last year I thought we were going to eat the rooster for dinner, but Abba sold it and gave the money to *tzedakah,* just like Uncle Meyer."

I'm glad a rooster or a hen is used for *kapparos,* but not a dove!

Bina and Benny's house is ready for Yom Kippur. The table is set with a white cloth and wine and *challah*, just like it is on Shabbos. But there is one difference. Tonight the family is eating before the holiday begins, and not afterwards.

"You can remove your leather shoes and put on your rubber or plastic shoes after we finish eating," said Abba.

"And you'll take your white *kittel* to *shul*," said Bina.

"And my white *tallis*! And just before Imma lights the candles, Imma and I have a special, once-a-year Yom Kippur *berachah* for you and Benny."

Yom Kippur is about to begin. Bina and Benny and Abba and Imma walk quickly but quietly on their way to *shul.* As they pass their neighbors, they smile and nod and say, "*Gemar chasimah tovah* — May your name be sealed in the Book of Life." There's no laughing or shouting or running tonight.

he *shul* is crowded with people. It looks like a gathering of angels, all dressed in clean, pure white. Each person hopes that G-d will forgive him or her for all of last year's sins. Each of us prays that G-d will seal our names in His Book of Life.

Before *Kol Nidrei*, *Sifrei Torah* are carried around the *shul* so that everyone can touch and kiss them.

Shhh. . .it's time for the *chazzan* to begin *Kol Nidrei:*

> *Al daas Hamakom* . . . and with the approval of the congregation . . . we allow the people to pray with those who have sinned.
>
> **Kol nidrei,** *ve'esoray, ushevuay . . .*

The *chazzan* sings each word slowly and carefully, asking and pleading with G-d, as the men and women and children listen and cry and say the words after him. Three times the *chazzan* repeats the prayer — softly, then just a little louder, and then in a full, loud voice — while the people sway back and forth as they whisper the words along with the *chazzan.*

> *V'nislach l'chol adas Bnei Yisrael* . . . May the entire congregation of the Children of Israel be forgiven . . .
>
> Forgive the sins of this people, as you

have forgiven them since the time of Egypt until now . . .

ow many *tefillos* are there on Yom Kippur, Benny?"

"There are five. *Maariv* at night. That's one. In the morning, *Shacharis* and *Mussaf*. That's three. In the afternoon there's *Minchah*. That's four. And right before the day is over, we have an extra *tefillah* — *Neilah*. That's five. So get ready for a long day!"

The *Kohen Gadol* — the High Priest — had a long day in the *Beis Hamikdash* on Yom Kippur. All night long he was awake learning Torah, and at the crack of dawn, he began the day. The *Avodah* — the service of the *Kohen Gadol* — atoned for the sins of all the people. The *Avodah* was a pretty big job, and it took every minute of the day to get it all done!

Just think! There were fifteen different sacrifices for the *Kohen Gadol* to bring. And he went to the *mikveh* and changed his clothes five separate times. And he entered the *Kodesh Kadashim* — the holiest part of the *Beis Hamikdash* — four times, the only times of the year when anyone was allowed in!

There were thousands and thousands of people in Yerushalayim on Yom Kippur. They filled the courtyard of the *Beis Hamikdash.* It was so crowded, they could hardly stand. Yet when they bowed down, there was suddenly room enough for everyone, just as if they were angels, not people!

The *Kohen Gadol* tied a red wool cord on the horns of a special goat, and when the red wool turned white, the people knew that *Hashem* had forgiven them for all of their sins.

"How sad that we don't have a *Kohen Gadol* or the *Beis Hamikdash* anymore," said Bina.

"But we have our *machzor,* full of prayers," said Benny. "And now G-d accepts our prayers in place of the sacrifices the Jews once brought."

ow do you feel, Bina?"

"I'm fine, Benny. How are you?"

"Well, I'm getting a little hungry. It's hard to go without breakfast and lunch."

"But it's only twelve o'clock! We thought we'd be able to wait until *Mussaf* is over before we eat. That's at least another two hours."

"Oiy! That's so long!"

"Why don't you think about the *Asarah Harugei Malchus* — the Ten Martyrs — instead of thinking about your stomach? They really suffered!" said Bina.

"I know," said a slightly shamefaced Benny. "But they were such great and holy rabbis and teachers. How could I ever be like them? The Romans tortured them to death, yet not a single one complained. Each and every one died *al kiddush Hashem* — for the holiness of G-d's name!"

"Maybe we can't be like them, but we can at least learn their names," said Bina.

"I did learn their names," said Benny.

"They are. . .

Rabbi Yishmael Kohen Gadol
Rabbi Shimon ben Gamliel
Rabbi Akiva
Rabbi Chaninah ben Teradyon
Rabbi Chutzpis Hameturgeman
Rabbi Elazar ben Shamua
Rabbi Chaninah ben Chachinai
Rabbi Yesheivav Hasofer
Rabbi Yehudah ben Dama
Rabbi Yehudah ben Bava

"And what about the story of Yonah we'll read during *Minchah* in the afternoon? Did you learn that too?"

"Of course I did," said Benny. "But let Chaggai tell it anyway."

ong ago in the Land of Israel, there lived a prophet by the name of Yonah ben Amitai. G-d commanded Yonah to go to the city of Nineveh in the land of Assyria to warn the people to do *teshuvah* and change their evil ways. If they would not listen, G-d would overturn the city. But Yonah did not want to go to Nineveh. He did not want to help the enemies of the Jews do *teshuvah.* And so he boarded a ship in order to run away from the Land of Israel, to a land far from Nineveh.

But *Hashem* caused a terrible storm to blow and churn up the sea. The ship was tossed from side to side, and the sailors were afraid. Each one prayed to his own idol, asking to be saved. Only Yonah was fast asleep — until the captain woke him up!

"Who are you?" he asked. "Get up and pray to your G-d."

"My G-d has made the heavens and the earth," he said, "and He has sent this storm to punish me. Throw me into the water and the storm will stop."

The sailors did not want to hurt Yonah, but they didn't want to drown either. So they threw Yonah overboard and the waves grew still. But Yonah didn't drown. G-d sent a huge fish to swallow him. For three days and three nights, Yonah lay in the deep, dark sea — inside the belly of the fish.

He understood that he had disobeyed *Hashem* and that he was being punished. He understood that he could not run away from G-d and that he must go to Nineveh as G-d had commanded. So Yonah prayed to *Hashem* from the bottom of the sea and the fish spit him safely up onto the dry land.

Yonah arrived in Nineveh and warned the people: "In forty days, Nineveh shall be turned over!"

The people of Nineveh believed Yonah. Everyone, even the king himself, did *teshuvah*! They fasted and wore clothes of mourning and sat on ashes. Even the animals were not given food or water. The people in the city prayed to G-d and promised to be good. They returned whatever they had stolen. Therefore, *Hashem* had pity on them and did not destroy the city.

But Yonah was unhappy. He complained to G-d. "I knew You would have pity on them," he said. "I would rather have died than to have helped these evil enemies of Israel!"

As Yonah sat outside the city waiting to see what would happen, G-d made a *kikayon* — a plant with large, shady leaves — grow nearby. Yonah was very pleased. He sat in the cool shade of the *kikayon* and watched the city of Nineveh. But the next day, *Hashem* sent a worm to gnaw at the plant. As quickly as it had grown, it withered

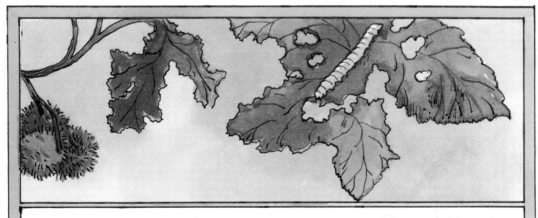

and died. Then G-d sent a hot east wind to blow on Yonah and the broiling sun beat down on his head.

"How miserable I am!" cried Yonah. "My life is no longer worth living!"

"Are you so sorry that the *kikayon* died?" asked *Hashem.*

"Yes," answered Yonah. "I am sorry enough to want to die myself."

"Yonah!" said G-d. "If you feel so sorry about a little plant which you did not create or take care of, something which grew up overnight, all by itself, shall I not feel sorry for the great city of Nineveh with all the people and children and animals which I have created?"

Yonah understood that *Hashem* is always ready to forgive, and anyone, anywhere, can always do *teshuvah.* And that, of course, is the reason we read the story of Yonah on Yom Kippur!

om Kippur is almost over, Benny."

"I know. The sun is setting. It's time for *Neilah.* In just a few minutes the day will end and the Gates of Heaven will close. In just a few minutes, G-d will make His final decisions for the New Year."

"*Hashem* really does want our names to be sealed in His Book of Life. That's why He gave us *Neilah* — a fifth, extra prayer as a last, extra chance to show we're really sorry for anything bad we've done this past year. I davened so carefully this Yom Kippur! I tried to say every single word. I hope my *tefillos* will help our family have a good year." Bina looked concerned.

"I'm sure they will, Bina. Don't worry. *Hashem* knows you tried your hardest. I just hope I didn't spoil my chances for a good year by teasing you so much all year long!"

Bina looked at her brother and smiled. Of course Benny's name would be sealed in the Book of Life! Benny was a wonderful brother and she was sure *Hashem* knew it, even if Benny did make her angry once in a while.

"The end of *Neilah* is my favorite part of Yom Kippur," said Benny. "We say all of my favorite *tefillos,* the ones I know by heart — *Shema Yisrael, Baruch Sheym Kevod Malchuso, Hashem Hu HaElokim,* and *Leshanah Haba'ah BeYirushalayim!*"

"And don't forget the *shofar,*" added Bina. "We end Yom Kippur with a big, long *tekiah gedolah* on the *shofar!*"

The very first Yom Kippur I'm in Jerusalem, I'm going to blow the *shofar* at the *Kosel!* I bet I'm related to the doves who live in the cracks and crannies in the Wall. Hmm. . . I wonder if someone puts out a dish of birdseed for them at the end of the day. . .

om Kippur is over. All around the world, Jews have finished a long day of fasting and praying. They are tired, but joyful. They trust that *Hashem* has heard their prayers and has sealed their names in His Book of Life. Before going home, they gather together outside their synagogues and *shuls* and *shteibels* and *batei knesses* to say *Birkas Halevanah* — the blessing on the moon.

Bina and Benny and their parents have just finished eating a happy, delicious, after-Yom Kippur meal. They are full of energy and ready for a very special *mitzvah.* In five days, the holiday of Succos will begin, but Bina and Benny's family isn't going to wait until the last minute. They are going out to the yard to start building their *succah* — right now!

GLOSSARY

aveirah — sin; opposite of *mitzvah*

batei knesses — synagogues

Beis Hamikdash — the Holy Temple in Jerusalem

berachah, berachos — blessing, blessings

challah — bread baked especially for the Sabbath and holidays

daven — pray

Eretz Yisrael — the Land of Israel

Erev Yom Kippur — the day before Yom Kippur

Har Sinai — Mt. Sinai

Hashem — G-d

kittel (Yiddish) — a white robe worn by married men on Yom Kippur

luchos — the stone tablets with the Ten Commandments

Maariv — the evening prayer

machzor — holiday prayer book

mechilah — forgiveness

mikveh — a pool for ritual immersion

Minchah — the afternoon prayer

mitzvah, mitzvos — a commandment, commandments

Moshe Rabbeinu — Moses our teacher

Mussaf — the additional Sabbath or holiday prayer

parashah — a portion of the Torah

Shabbos — the Sabbath

Shacharis — the morning prayer

shteibel (Yiddish) — a small synagogue

shul (Yiddish) — synagogue

Sifrei Torah — Torah Scrolls

tallis — prayer shawl

tefillah, tefillos — prayer, prayers

teshuvah — being sorry and deciding to do better

tzedakah — charity

Yerushalayim — Jerusalem

Yonah — the prophet Jonah